YOU BE THE JURY

Courtroom II

Also by
MARVIN MILLER:

YOU BE THE JURY

Courtroom II

Marvin Miller

Inside illustrations by Bob Roper

SCHOLASTIC INC.

New York Toronto London Auckland Sydney

ISBN 0-590-45725-X

Copyright © 1989 by Marvin Miller.
All rights reserved. Published by Scholastic Inc.

12 11 10 9 8   6 7/9

Printed in the U.S.A.   40

. . for Robby, again . . . .

CONTENTS

Order in the Court

LADIES AND GENTLEMEN OF THE JURY:

This court is now in session. My name is Judge John Dennenberg. You are the jury, and the trials are set to begin.

You have a serious responsibility. Will the innocent be sent to jail and the guilty go free? Let's hope not. Your job is to make sure that justice is served.

Read each case carefully. Study the evidence presented and then decide:

GUILTY OR NOT GUILTY??

Both sides of the case will be presented to you. The person who has the complaint is called the *plaintiff*. He or she has brought the case to court. If a crime is involved, the State is the accuser.

The person being accused is called the *defendant*. The defendant is pleading his or her innocence and presents a much different version of what happened.

IN EACH CASE, THREE PIECES OF EVIDENCE WILL BE PRESENTED AS

1

EXHIBITS A, B, AND C. EXAMINE THE EXHIBITS VERY CAREFULLY. A *CLUE* TO THE SOLUTION OF EACH CASE WILL BE FOUND THERE. IT WILL DIRECTLY POINT TO THE INNOCENCE OR GUILT OF THE ACCUSED.

Remember, each side will try to convince you that his or her version is what actually happened. BUT YOU MUST MAKE THE FINAL DECISION.

The Case of the Flying Toy

LADIES AND GENTLEMEN OF THE JURY:

When a person invents something, that invention can be legally protected. The inventor fills out an application, and if the invention is found to be original, the United States Patent Office sends the inventor an official document called a patent. This prevents other people from using the inventor's idea.

The case you are asked to judge today involves a patented toy called SPIRALWIZ. This unusual flying toy has been sold worldwide by Backwards Industries, Incorporated.

Last year, Andrew Dobbs, who is the owner of a small plastics company, began selling an identical toy. He named it FLYFLIP.

Backwards Industries, the plaintiff, has asked the court to stop Andrew Dobbs from selling FLYFLIP because it is a copy of their invention. But Mr. Dobbs, the defendant, claims that his grandfather invented FLYFLIP 30 years ago, long before Backwards Industries had the idea.

A scientist for Backwards Industries has given the following testimony:

"My name is Dr. Robert Franklin. You might think that all scientists are nerdy people who walk around carrying test tubes and never have any fun, but at Backwards Industries we're not like that. In fact, my job is to sit around all day and think up ideas for new toys. I invented SPIRALWIZ for Backwards Industries.

"SPIRALWIZ is one of the most unusual floating toys ever invented. When you fling it in the air, it travels straight ahead. Then it rises skyward, flips upside down, and floats gently back into your hand."

EXHIBIT A is a photograph of this amazing toy.

As proof that SPIRALWIZ is an original invention, Backwards Industries also submitted EXHIBIT B. This is the patent issued to the scientist from Backwards Industries who claims to have invented SPIRALWIZ.

Andrew Dobbs challenges Backwards Industries. In claiming that the toy was an old idea of his grandfather's, he offers the following testimony:

"As a boy, I remember Gramps telling me about his idea for a toy that would fly back into the hands of the person who threw it. He was working on it for a long time. Then he surprised me one day when he brought home this fantastic gadget.

"We went out in the yard and he showed me how it worked. We took turns throwing the toy in

4

the air. We played with it the whole afternoon. But Gramps had no idea of ever selling it as a product. He just worked on his ideas for the fun of it. In fact, the next day he was busy working on another invention, musical gum that plays a tune as you chew it."

While no one else saw Gramps' toy, Andrew Dobbs claims that his grandfather kept careful records. He had notebooks for all his inventions and they were stored in the attic when the old man died.

Mr. Dobbs located his grandfather's notes. EXHIBIT C is the last page of the notebook that shows a drawing of the toy. You will observe that the sketch is identical to SPIRALWIZ that Backwards Industries claims to have invented.

No one saw a working model of Gramps' toy besides Andrew Dobbs. But Mr. Dobbs offers the testimony of a friend who knew of his grandfather's experiments.

"My name is Charlie Watson. Gramps Dobbs was a good friend of mine. I know, I know. . . . You think it's funny that I called him Gramps when we weren't even related. But that's what everybody called him. I spent a lot of time with him when he was working on that crazy toy idea.

"Every day, for three weeks, I drove him to a remote field on the outskirts of town. Gramps didn't want anyone to see him working on his invention. To reach the field, we had to drive down a long, bumpy road that few people in town knew.

"I never bothered Gramps while he was trying to get the toy to work. I just went digging in the road, looking for unusual rocks for my geology collection. The road was covered with stones and rocks of all kinds. I used to find a lot of garnet and tourmaline.

"I clearly remember the last day we went to the field together. I was busy examining a large boulder when Gramps ran over to me very excited. He said he finally got his flying invention to work.

"But Gramps wouldn't show me the toy. He was very secretive about all his inventions.

"As we drove home, Gramps began writing in his notebook. He wouldn't even show me what he was writing. Then he slammed the notebook shut. He said, 'I'm glad that's finished. It took a long time to get that toy to work. Now on to my next invention.'"

"A lawyer for Backwards Industries claims the drawing in EXHIBIT C is a fake. He has stated:

"Except for the sketch on the last page, the notebook contains no written description of the invention — or statement that it even worked. There are no other drawings in the notebook.

"In fact, in this notebook, Grandfather Dobbs wrote about his experiments that failed. He never wrote that he could get the toy to work properly. And it seems strange that he would not show the invention to his friend, Charlie Watson. Could he have been ashamed that he had failed to get his toy to work?

"No, old Mr. Dobbs never got his flying toy to work. In fact, we believe his grandson Andrew Dobbs really drew the sketch himself. He knew he would have to stop selling FLYFLIP if Backwards Industries could prove to the court that the invention was theirs."

LADIES AND GENTLEMEN OF THE JURY:
You have just heard the Case of the Flying Toy. You must decide the merit of Backwards Industries' claim. Be sure to carefully examine EXHIBITS A, B, and C.

Was Grandfather Dobbs the original inventor of the flying toy? Or was the drawing in his notebook a fake?

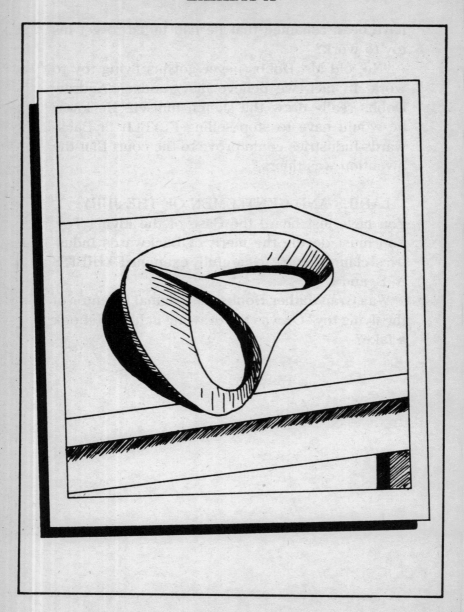

EXHIBIT B

United States Patent Office

138,644
FLYING TOY
Robert Franklin, Freethrow, CA, assignor to
Backwards Industries, Inc., Freethrow, CA
Filed July 17, 1985, Ser. No. 21,655

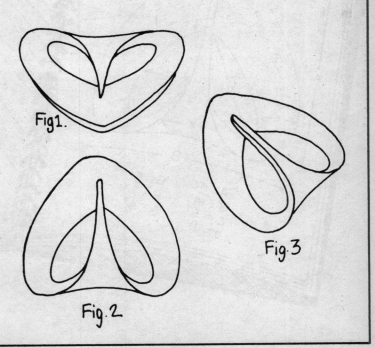

Fig 1.

Fig. 2.

Fig. 3

9

EXHIBIT C

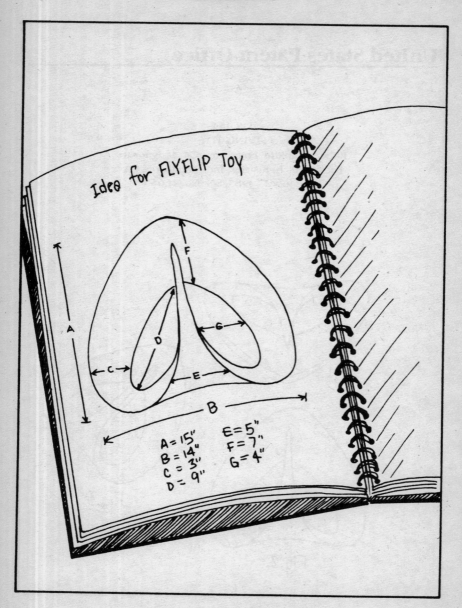

VERDICT

THE DRAWING IN THE NOTEBOOK WAS A FAKE.

Charlie Watson testified that Grandpa Dobbs wrote the last page in his notebook while they were driving down a long, bumpy road. But the drawing and handwriting on the page are smooth and even, as though they had been written at a desk. Andrew Dobbs had added the final page himself.

The Case
of the Troublesome Twins

Ladies AND GENTLEMEN OF THE JURY:

For a person to be found guilty of a crime, there must be sufficient proof that he was the one who committed it.

Keep this in mind as you go over the facts of this very unusual case.

Farmer Foley, the plaintiff, accuses Bart Lee of breaking the lock on his chicken coop door. All the chickens escaped. He is suing Bart Lee for the amount of money it will take to replace the chickens.

Bart Lee, the defendant, claims he is not guilty of the crime since Farmer Foley cannot say for certain whether it was he or his twin brother who did it. If there is not enough evidence to point to either twin, then neither can be found guilty.

Farmer Foley has testified as follows:

"One rainy afternoon, April 19 to be exact, as I was sitting on the porch of my house, I saw a figure sneaking onto the far side of my property. The person was holding something that looked like a large stick.

"As I rose from my rocking chair, I saw the

intruder banging away at the chicken coop door. Seconds later, the vandal pulled the door open and the chickens rushed out, scurrying in all directions."

Farmer Foley chased the intruder through the muddy grounds. As he gained on him, the figure suddenly tripped and fell. When the person picked himself up, Foley grabbed him by the collar and marched him into the house.

The intruder turned out to be a young man of about nineteen years. He refused to identify himself. Despite the youth's pleas, Farmer Foley telephoned the police.

As they waited for the police to arrive, the intruder telephoned his brother and asked that he meet him at police headquarters.

When the police brought the intruder to the station, the young man was permitted to go into the next room to give his keys and money to his brother.

Minutes later, when the young man walked out of the room, the officer booked him for the crime. The youth said his name was Bart Lee, but he claimed he was innocent. And when his brother came out of the next room, he also claimed his innocence. To everyone's surprise, the brothers were identical twins!

While in the next room, the brothers had exchanged some of their clothing. They had purposely confused everyone.

I will now read from the testimony of the arresting officer. First the question and then his answer:

Q: How can you be sure that Bart Lee is the same twin you arrested?

A: Well, he was the first one out of the room. And he was wearing the same striped shirt as the guy I arrested at the farm.

Q: Was he wearing all the same clothing as the person you caught at the farm?

A: No. He had on some of his brother's clothes.

Q: What else was the person you arrested at the farm wearing?

A: I didn't notice everything. But he had on a dark jacket and dark-colored pants when I caught him.

Q: And what about the shirt he was wearing?

A: Yes, he had a striped shirt . I could see part of it under his jacket. And he had on sandals without socks.

The muddy ground around the chicken coop provided an important piece of evidence. This is shown in EXHIBIT A. Whoever broke into the coop left a trail of footprints behind.

EXHIBIT B is one of the sandals worn by the first twin to come out of the room . He identified himself as Bart Lee and is the twin who was booked for the crime. As you will note, an imprint of the sandal Bart was wearing exactly matches the footprints found around the chicken coop.

The arresting officer continued with his testimony as follows:

Q: What happened when you arrived with the vandal at police headquarters?

A: He asked my permission to go into the next room.

Q: Why did you let him?

A: Well, the kid seemed really scared. I figured his brother would quiet him down. But I didn't know that he had a *twin* brother in there.

Q: How long was he in the other room?

A: Only for a few minutes.

Q: Was it enough time for them to switch shirts, pants, and shoes?

A: I don't know.

EXHIBIT C is a photograph of both twins taken at the police station. One is wearing a light jacket and dark pants while the other has a dark jacket and light pants. Both have a shirt underneath. The twin on the left is Bart Lee, the one who was booked for the crime. He is wearing a striped shirt.

The lawyer for Farmer Foley raises an important question:

"Even though the brothers switched some of their clothing, why did the twin who was first to leave the room allow himself to be booked? That is, unless he really is the guilty one?

"Surely common sense argues that the twin who left the room first, and who is on trial here today, has to be the guilty party."

LADIES AND GENTLEMEN OF THE JURY:
You have just heard the Case of the Troublesome Twins. You are to decide the merit of Farmer Foley's accusation. Be sure to carefully examine the evidence in EXHIBITS A, B, C.

Was Bart Lee guilty of breaking open Farmer Foley's chicken coop? Or did his twin brother do it?

EXHIBIT B

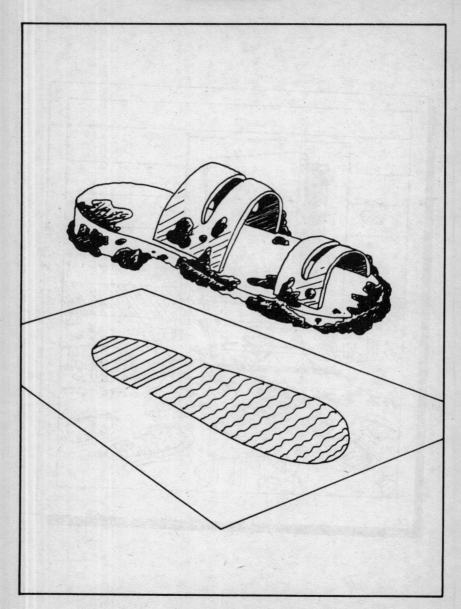

EXHIBIT C

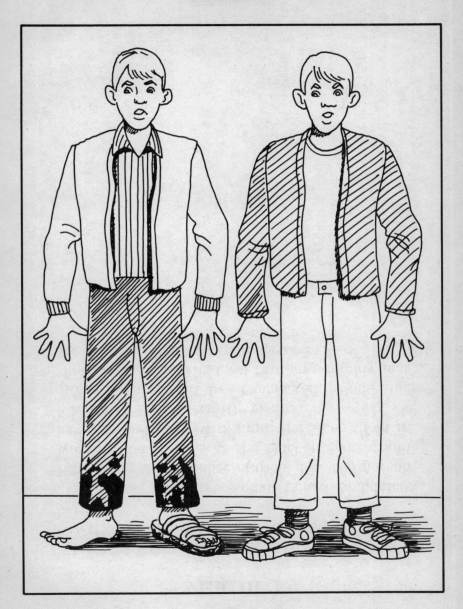

VERDICT

BART LEE WAS INNOCENT. HIS TWIN BROTHER WAS THE GUILTY ONE.

EXHIBIT B shows the mud-stained sandal that Bart wore at the police station. But the person wearing the sandals at the chicken coop would have his feet filthy with mud. Bart Lee's feet in EXHIBIT C are perfectly clean.

The clothing Bart Lee exchanged included his shoes and socks. His twin brother's muddy feet are inside Bart's socks and sneakers.

20

The Case of
the Sleeping Prisoner

LADIES AND GENTLEMEN OF THE JURY:

Escape from jail is a serious crime, even if the person was arrested for a minor offense.

Such is the case before you today. Since we are in criminal court, the State is the accuser.

The State contends that Soney Najac, who was arrested for sleeping on a park bench, broke out of jail. But Mr. Najac claims his cell door was unlocked. He just pushed it open and walked out.

The patrolman, Thomas Nash, testifies as follows:

"It was about two o'clock in the morning and I was making my rounds in Vernon Park. No one is supposed to be there after dark.

"I was walking along when I heard a strange sound. At first I thought it might be thunder, but it was a starry night without any clouds. Then I realized what the sound was. Someone was snoring. I turned on my flashlight and there was this man on a bench. He was sound asleep.

"I tried to wake him but without success. I couldn't leave him there, so I figured the best thing

21

to do was to strap him onto my motorcycle and drive down to police headquarters."

The stranger's wallet provided more information. His name was Soney Najac and the address inside showed he was from a foreign country.

The patrolman continued his testimony:

"The man was still asleep when I got to the station, so I carried him into a cell. It was my turn for night duty and I relieved the officer in charge.

"About six o'clock that morning, I went to the coffee shop around the corner to bring back some coffee and donuts. It couldn't have taken more than a few minutes.

"When I got back, I was shocked to find the cell door open. The prisoner had escaped."

All police were alerted. That afternoon Soney Najac was arrested in the downtown area, while he was looking in a store window. This time it was a more serious charge: escaping from jail.

The State described its theory of how Mr. Najac managed his escape. EXHIBIT A is a diagram showing the inside of the police station. It has two jail cells. On a side wall is a box containing keys. Mr. Najac was in the cell nearest the wall.

Two close-up photographs showing the key box are presented as EXHIBIT B. They show the box both open and closed. Each key is hanging on a large ring. If someone in a cell had a long pole, it would be possible for him to reach the key box.

This, the State contends, is how the breakout occurred. It enters as EXHIBIT C a photograph showing a broom that was found near Soney Najac's cell.

The State believes that the prisoner grabbed the broom, reached over to the box, and caught the key ring on one end. This was his means of escape.

I will now read for the cross-examination of Patrolman Nash by Mr. Najac's court-appointed lawyer:

Q: How can you be sure the cell door was locked?

A: I have been a policeman in this town for fifteen years. In all that time I never left a cell unlocked. What makes anyone think I did it this time?

Q: Did you find the door to the key box closed following the prisoner's departure?

A: It had to be. The door is on a spring and it swings closed automatically.

Q: Then how was it possible for Mr. Najac to use the broom to loop the key?

A: That's not hard to do. The ring on the front of the box can be pulled open with the broom handle. Then you can quickly catch the big key ring on the end of the broom before the door shuts. I know it can be done. I've tried it myself.

Soney Najac testified on his own behalf. Since

he could not speak English, his testimony was presented through an interpreter.

"My name is Soney Najac. I arrived in your country just two weeks ago. A friend told me I might find a good job in this area. So I took a bus to your town.

"I was tired from the trip and didn't have much money. When it got dark, I walked into the park and saw a bench. I hadn't had much sleep for the past few days, so I lay down on the bench for the night.

"When I woke up, I didn't know where I was. All I knew was that I was in this room with bars. No one else was around.

"I stood up and leaned against the door. It started to move, so I pushed it open and walked out. I never knew I had been arrested."

Mr. Najac's lawyer continues his defense:

"As proof that Mr. Najac did not use a key to escape from his cell, your attention is again drawn to EXHIBIT B. This photograph was taken shortly after the alleged breakout occurred.

"You will note the keys to both cells are hanging on their hooks. If Mr. Najac had used the key to escape, he never would have taken the time to put it back on its hook.

"The State's theory of the escape is hard to believe. The truth is simply this: Soney Najac woke up, didn't know where he was, found the cell door open — and just walked out!"

LADIES AND GENTLEMEN OF THE JURY:
You have just heard the Case of the Sleeping Prisoner. You must decide the merit of the State's accusation. Be sure to carefully examine the evidence in EXHIBITS A, B, and C.

Did Soney Najac escape from jail using a key? Or did he walk out of the unlocked door?

EXHIBIT A

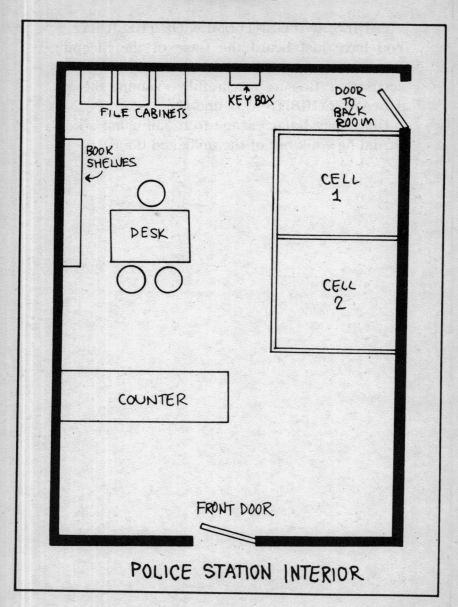

FILE CABINETS

KEY BOX

DOOR TO BACK ROOM

BOOK SHELVES

DESK

CELL 1

CELL 2

COUNTER

FRONT DOOR

POLICE STATION INTERIOR

EXHIBIT B

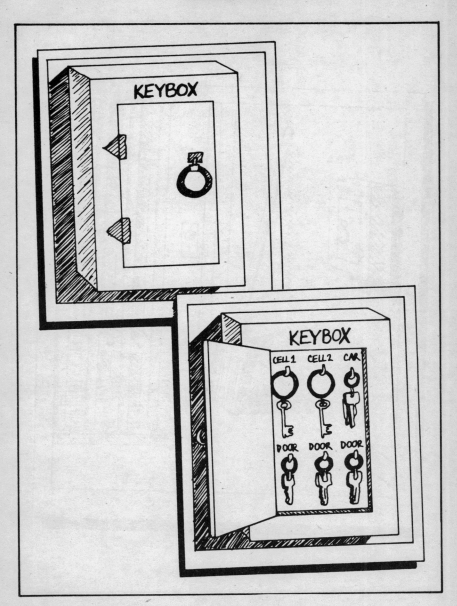

EXHIBIT C

VERDICT

THE CELL DOOR WAS NEVER LOCKED.

EXHIBIT B, on the left side, shows the key box as Soney Najac would have seen it when he awoke. Since he could not speak English, he could not have read the front of the box to know it contained the key to his cell.

The Case of
the High-Kicking Horse

Ladies and Gentlemen of the Jury:

If a horse owner does not properly train his horse and it injures someone, the owner is responsible.

Tom Clive, the plaintiff, allegedly was kicked in the head by a horse called Lightning. He suffered severe head injuries and is suing Howard Simm, the owner. He claims that if Lightning had been properly trained, the horse would not have kicked him. Howard Simm, the defendant, says that the horse was well trained.

Tom Clive has testified as follows:

"My name is Tom Clive. I'm a successful jockey who's worked for a number of the top horse owners in the country. I'm the best and I don't care who knows it. Maybe you saw me last year in the Kentucky Derby. Anyway, I was hired by Howard Simm to ride his horse Lightning in the Langdon Races.

"But the first day I was working out with Lightning, Mr. Simm walked up to me and fired me. Just like that! For no reason at all. He told me to get off his property and he'd send me my riding gear the next day.

"Well, I was so angry with Howard Simm that I decided I wasn't going to wait until the next day for my things. I wanted to clear out that night and never see the owner again.

"I snuck back to the stable around midnight. The light in the stable must have been out, so I felt my way to the rear of the stable and over to my locker. I grabbed my gear and headed for the door. Then I remembered I'd left my riding crop inside Lightning's stall.

"When I went to get my riding crop, Lightning was restless and neighing. As I opened the stall door, the horse reared its hind legs and began kicking. He caught me on my forehead. My head still hurts when I think about it.

"I must have been out for hours. When I awoke it was dawn. I could see that Lightning was inside his stall."

Thomas Clive's lawyer entered as EXHIBIT A a photograph of the stall as it appeared that morning.

He also entered as EXHIBIT B a photograph of the baseball hat Thomas Clive was wearing at the time he suffered the injury. Mr. Clive says the horseshoe mark on the hat shows where Lightning kicked him.

In his testimony, Howard Simm raised doubt about Clive's account of the accident. First the question and then his answer:

Q: Why do you question the facts of Tom Clive's story?

A: Well, I didn't like Clive's attitude from the start. I knew he had had trouble with other owners, but I decided to hire him anyway.

Q: What made you change your mind?

A: It was after Clive had his first workout with Lightning. He said my horse wasn't well trained. He called Lightning too wild to be a winner.

Q: Is that when you fired Mr. Clive?

A: Sure. I didn't want a person like him riding Lightning. So I told the jockey he was finished.

Q: What was his reaction?

A: He never expected me to fire him. When I told him I would get another jockey instead, Clive became very angry. He said I would regret it.

Howard Simm offered another explanation for the jockey's injury:

"I don't know why Tom Clive decided to pick up his riding things that night. I told him I'd send them the next day. He might have been trying to hurt Lightning.

"I can't say whether Lightning kicked the jockey or not. But if Clive was stupid enough to go into my stable after dark, he should have known it might be dangerous. Clive could have banged his head on anything. He would have had trouble walking through the stable in the dark."

He entered EXHIBIT C, a photograph of Tom Clive's locker, to prove his theory.

"Clive could easily have hit his head on that beam near his locker and used the accident to blame Lightning. He said he would get even with me. Maybe he even faked the whole thing.

"There are old horseshoes inside the barn. If Clive wanted to blame Lightning, all he had to do was find one and slam it into his baseball hat.

"You can't tell from the mark on Tom Clive's hat whether it was done by Lightning or not. Any old horseshoe could have done it."

LADIES AND GENTLEMEN OF THE JURY:
You have just heard the Case of the High-Kicking Horse. You must decide the merit of Tom Clive's claim. Be sure to carefully examine the evidence in EXHIBITS A, B, and C.

Did Lightning kick Tom Clive? Or did the jockey fake the accident?

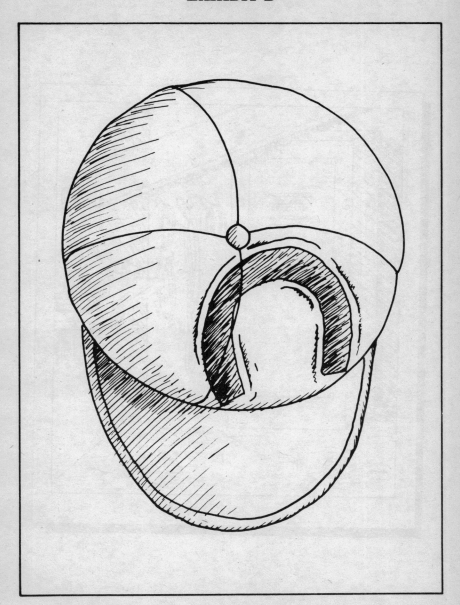

EXHIBIT C

VERDICT

TOM CLIVE FAKED THE HORSESHOE MARK ON HIS HAT.

The mark in EXHIBIT B shows the horseshoe had hit the hat with a downward blow. Clive overlooked the fact that horses kick *upward*. If Lightning had kicked him, the horseshoe mark would have been turned upside down with the round part on the bottom.

The Case of the Leaky Basement

LADIES AND GENTLEMEN OF THE JURY:

When an agreement is made in writing, it becomes a legal obligation.

This is the point of law you must keep in mind today.

George Clark, the plaintiff, agreed to buy a house from Lester Lyon for $94,000. Mr. Clark then wrote a letter to Lester Lyon confirming their agreement. He enclosed a $1,000 check as a deposit.

But Mr. Clark discovered the house was poorly built and withdrew his offer. He is suing Lester Lyon, the defendant, because Mr. Lyon won't return his deposit.

George Clark has testified as follows:

"When I first looked over Mr. Lyon's house, it seemed just what I wanted. I liked the layout and its location. I agreed to his selling price provided the house was inspected by a professional construction engineer. I didn't want any surprises after I bought it.

"Mr. Lyon told me he had others who wanted to purchase his house. He said that if I were serious about my offer, I should confirm it in writing and enclose a $1,000 deposit.

"I agreed, and sent him a letter the next day.

EXHIBIT A is the check George Clark sent to Mr. Lyon.

Mr. Clark hired a construction engineer to inspect the house. When the engineer brought the report to Mr. Clark's home, it was unsatisfactory. It seems Lyon's house was built on land that was once a swamp. A heavy rain could cause basement flooding. A real storm might even make the house float away. The engineer showed Mr. Clark a picture he had taken of watermarks in the basement.

When the engineer showed him the photograph, George Clark immediately telephoned the owner. He told Lyon their deal was off and requested that he return the $1,000.

"When I told Lester Lyon I was withdrawing my offer, he warned me that if I did, I wouldn't get back my deposit. And he told me I had agreed the money was his no matter what happened. He said I wrote that in the letter I sent him.

"I couldn't believe it. I certainly never wrote any such thing. I pulled out my checkbook to show the engineer that Lyon must have been mistaken. On the stub of the check I had written a note to myself that it was a 'refundable deposit.'

"The engineer took out his camera and photographed my checkbook. He said it would be important evidence if I ever had to go to court."

This photograph was entered as EXHIBIT B. The engineer has sworn under oath that he was with George during the telephone conversation.

Lester Lyon had a very different story to tell:

"When I put a notice in the newspaper advertising my house for sale, four people called to say they were interested. I decided to sell my house to Clark because he was the first to come over.

"When Mr. Clark and I agreed on the purchase price, I told him about the other people interested in buying it. I accepted his bid only when he agreed to send me the deposit. He knew he wouldn't get it back if he withdrew his offer."

George Clark's letter accompanying the check appears as EXHIBIT C. It proves that Mr. Clark's purchase of the house depended on the inspection by a professional engineer.

Mr. Lyon's attorney has called your attention to the note at the bottom of this letter. It clearly states that George Clark agreed that the deposit was not refundable.

Mr. Clark claims he wrote the top part of the letter in EXHIBIT C, but not the wording at the bottom. He accuses Lester Lyon of introducing false evidence into court. He claims Mr. Lyon added the bottom section after he received George Clark's letter.

Lester Lyon was able to get another buyer for his house. It was sold at the same price as George

Clark's offer. But he refuses to return the $1,000.

LADIES AND GENTLEMEN OF THE JURY:
You have just heard the Case of the Leaky Basement. You must decide the merit of George Clark's claim. Be sure to carefully examine the evidence in EXHIBITS A, B, and C.

Can Lester Lyon keep the $1,000 deposit? Or did he add the wording to George Clark's letter?

EXHIBIT A

GEORGE CLARK
503 BENNET DR.
HANOVER, NC. 10321

1426

October 12, 19 88

Pay to the order of ___Lester Lynn___ $ 1,000 xx

___One thousand and 100/xx___ ~~~~~~~~~~~~~~~ Dollars

RIGIDITY
BANK

for ___Deposit___   George Clark

02170032

42

CHECK NO.	DATE	CHECK TO	AMOUNT	BALANCE
1425	10/11	CASH	100.00	1,510.00
1426	10/12	LESTER LYON REFUNDABLE DEPOSIT	1000.00	510.00

EXHIBIT C

G E O R G E   C L A R K

October 12, 1988

Mr. Lester Lyon
857 Front St.
Hanover, N.C.

Dear Mr. Lyon:

Confirming our meeting yesterday, I wish to acknowledge my interest in purchasing your house for $94,000.00. This purchase is subject to satisfactory inspection by a professional builder.

As you requested, enclosed is a check for $1,000.00 as a deposit.

Sincerely,

George Clark

PS. **I understand that the $1,000.00 deposit is not refundable to me.**

VERDICT

LESTER LYON TYPED THE BOTTOM OF THE LETTER.

The bottom sentence of the letter in EXHIBIT C contains asterisks. But the photograph in exhibit B shows that George Clark's typewriter does not have an asterisk key. It could not have been typed on Clark's typewriter.

The Case of
the Missing Ring

LADIES AND GENTLEMEN OF THE JURY:

Grand larceny is a very serious crime. It is the theft of something worth a great deal of money.

Dora Watson, the plaintiff, has accused Fritz Lindsay of breaking into her bedroom and stealing her expensive diamond ring. Fritz Lindsay, the defendant, states that the ring was never stolen. He claims it was lost by Mrs. Watson. He found it in a movie theater the same evening she was there.

Mrs. Watson has testified as follows:

"On Saturday evening, July 8, my husband and I went out to see a movie. Our daughter Jennifer was baby-sitting for our three-year-old son.

"When we returned home late that evening, I realized the ring was not on my finger. But I thought I had just forgotten to put it on when I dressed for the theater. I searched frantically in our bedroom, but I couldn't find the ring anywhere.

"When I couldn't find the ring at home, I figured I must have worn it to the theater and it had fallen off my finger that evening. It had been a little loose and I had meant to get it tightened. I called Blake

Theater to see if anyone had found a ring. But no one had reported it."

Mrs. Watson's daughter stated that while she was baby-sitting the evening her parents went out, she heard a strange noise in their bedroom. When she went upstairs to check, nothing seemed wrong. But as she looked out the bedroom window, she saw a man walking across the lawn of their house. Jennifer didn't think much of it until her mother said the ring was missing.

Mrs. Watson placed an ad in the paper offering a reward to anyone finding her diamond ring. This advertisement is entered as EXHIBIT A.

The day the ad appeared, Fritz Lindsay came to the Watson house. He explained to Mrs. Watson that he had been in the Blake Theater the same evening that she was. He was one of the last to leave and had found a ring on the floor in a corner of the lobby.

Fritz Lindsay removed a diamond ring from his pocket and asked Mrs. Watson if she could identify it. Mrs. Watson was thrilled. Her ring had been found. She gladly offered to pay Lindsay the reward money.

This diamond ring is entered as EXHIBIT B.

During all the excitement, Jennifer whispered to her father that Fritz Lindsay looked just like the man she had seen walking across the lawn that Saturday evening. Mr. Watson slipped into the kitchen and called the police.

While Fritz Lindsay was still at the Watson home, the police arrived. They arrested him for the theft of Mrs. Watson's diamond ring. He is charged here today with grand larceny.

The lawyer for the defense claimed that the identification of Fritz Lindsay was a case of mistaken identity. At the time Jennifer looked out the bedroom window, it was very late at night. It would have been difficult to see clearly the person who was in her backyard.

Fritz Lindsay testified as follows:

"I was nowhere near the Watson house that night. When I saw the ad in the paper, I thought it might be talking about the ring I found. I was only trying to do a good deed."

Mr. Lindsay provided proof that he was at the theater the same night as Mr. and Mrs. Watson. While he could not produce a witness who saw him, he entered as evidence a torn ticket stub from the movie. This is shown in EXHIBIT C.

The management of Blake Theater acknowledged that the stub was from a ticket purchased on the same Saturday the Watsons went to the theater. But they were unable to verify the exact time it was bought.

Fritz Lindsay continued his testimony:

"When the movie was over I stopped at a vending machine to buy some candy. As I was eating it, I saw something shiny in the corner. To my surprise, I discovered it was an expensive ring. The manager of the theater wasn't around and I didn't want to leave it with anyone else. So I took the ring home.

"I never stole any ring. I found it in the theater and that reward money is mine."

LADIES AND GENTLEMEN OF THE JURY:
You have just heard the Case of the Missing Ring. You must decide the merits of Dora Watson's accusation. Be sure to carefully examine the evidence in EXHIBITS A, B, and C.

Did Fritz Lindsay steal Mrs. Watson's ring? Or did he find it at the Blake Theater?

EXHIBIT A

ANNOUNCEMENTS

ATTENTION DIETERS
Try new Tropical Treat diet. All you eat is pineapple. Saves you money. Call 505-3000.

LOST BANK BOOK
01-342-7-5020
If found please return to
H. Hughes, Las Vegas, Nevada.

REWARD
For return of diamond ring lost in or near Blake Theater on July 8.
Contact: P.O. Box 352
Harmony, N.Y. 17834

PUPPET SHOWS
Lifelike entertainment for parties. These puppets look so real . . . maybe they are!
Call M. Giappetto, 355-1212.

EXHIBIT C

VERDICT

FRITZ LINDSAY STOLE THE RING.

The ad in EXHIBIT A contains a post office box number, not Mrs. Watson's address. Lindsay could not have known where the owner of the ring lived unless he had stolen it from her house.

The Case of
the Broken Display Case

LADIES AND GENTLEMEN OF THE JURY:

When a person on trial for a crime cannot be positively identified, then the court may rely on circumstantial evidence. Circumstantial evidence is a group of facts that can lead the jury to decide if a person is guilty or innocent. There must be enough evidence to prove a person guilty beyond a shadow of a doubt.

The State has accused Edward Carlson, the defendant, of breaking the glass display case in the Sheridan School gym with the intent to steal a valuable trophy. Mr. Carlson claims he is innocent of the crime.

The State called Steven Stone, the Sheridan School principal, to the witness stand:

"Every year during spring vacation, Sheridan School holds its annual fair. This year the money we raised was used to buy new equipment for the soccer team.

"The fair is a major event. Everyone in the community looks forward to it. There are booths with games of chance and skill. Other booths have food and student crafts for sale.

"The fair is held in the school gym. This year Edward Carlson, a cafeteria worker, volunteered to be in charge of the bowling booth.

"At six o'clock on the evening before the fair, I was about to leave the school for the night. As I passed the gym, I heard a strange noise inside. When I opened the door I could see someone at the far end of the gym, standing over the display case. He was holding a large object raised over his head.

"Before I could yell for him to stop, he smashed the top of the display case with the object."

EXHIBIT A is a photograph of the broken display case. The sterling silver trophy inside was untouched. The principal had interrupted the intruder before he was able to remove it.

The principal continued his testimony:

"I chased the intruder and he ran into the boys' locker room. I was right behind him. From the locker room he ran into the gym office and then out a rear door. He was running too fast for me to catch him."

The principal was unable to see the face of the intruder, but he described him as a male, approximately six feet tall and wearing a white T-shirt, dark pants, and sneakers.

When the principal returned to the gym office,

he noticed a bowling pin lying on the floor. It looked like the object used to break the display case. It was turned over to police and examined for fingerprints.

The pin, with its print marks, is entered as EXHIBIT B. Because the bowling pin was scratched from use, it is impossible to tell for sure if it was the object used to smash the display case.

The police determined the prints on the bowling pin match those of Edward Carlson. Further investigation has shown the defendant has a criminal record of petty larceny (or small thefts). A record of his arrest and his fingerprint file are shown as EXHIBIT C.

The testimony of Edward Carlson was then presented. First the question and then his answer:

Q: Where were you at six o'clock on the evening before the fair?

A: I finished setting up the bowling booth and left school around four o'clock. At six o'clock I was in my apartment watching television.

Q: Was there anyone with you who can verify that you were in your apartment at the time in question?

A: I live alone with my dog, Mutt. I don't remember anyone seeing me enter that night.

Q: Does that mean you have no one who can verify your whereabouts at six o'clock?

A: No one saw me.

Q: How do you account for your fingerprints on the bowling pin?

A: Sure they are my prints. I picked up a bunch of bowling pins from the supply closet in the gym office. They were for the fair booth. I made two trips to the office. One was for the bowling balls and the other for the pins.

Q: But why was the bowling pin in EXHIBIT B found on the gym office floor?

A: My arms were full. I must have dropped one while I was carrying them to the gym.

Q: If you dropped a bowling pin, why didn't you pick it up?

A: I never actually heard a pin fall. But one must have dropped. That's the only way I can explain it being on the office floor. There was banging and sawing going on in the gym. Other people were setting up their booths. There was too much noise to hear a bowling pin drop.

The defense claims that since the principal never saw the intruder drop a bowling pin as he chased him, there is no way to prove the pin on the office floor was the object used to break the display case.

The State claims that since the bowling pin found on the office floor bears the fingerprints of Edward Carlson, then it is logical to conclude that he was the intruder and that he dropped the pin as he was chased by the principal.

LADIES AND GENTLEMEN OF THE JURY:
You have just heard the Case of the Broken Display Case. You must decide the merits of the State's claim. Be sure to carefully examine the evidence in EXHIBITS A, B, and C.

Was Edward Carlson the person who smashed the display case? Or was the intruder someone else?

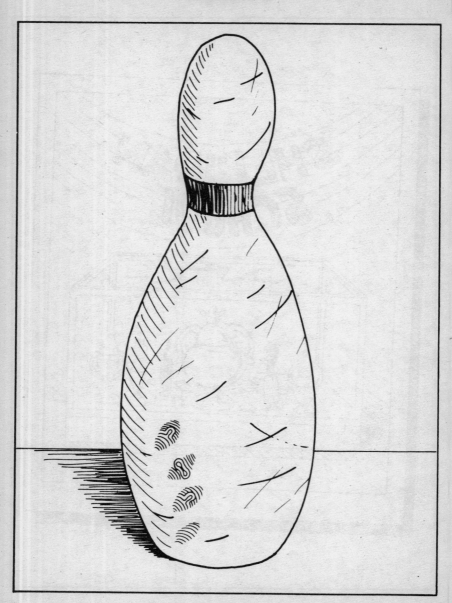

EXHIBIT C

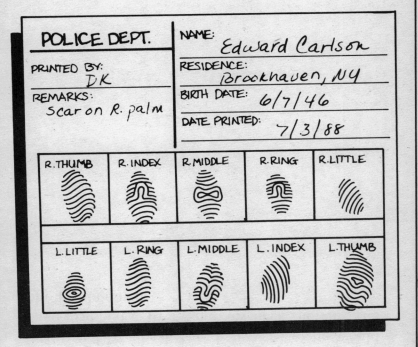

POLICE DEPT.

PRINTED BY:
DK

REMARKS:
Scar on R. palm

NAME:
Edward Carlson

RESIDENCE:
Brookhaven, NY

BIRTH DATE: 6/7/46

DATE PRINTED: 7/3/88

R. THUMB	R. INDEX	R. MIDDLE	R. RING	R. LITTLE

L. LITTLE	L. RING	L. MIDDLE	L. INDEX	L. THUMB

VERDICT

EDWARD CARLSON WAS NOT GUILTY.

The fingerprints in EXHIBIT B show how Carlson had grabbed the bowling pin. He held the wide part of the pin. If the bowling pin had been used to smash the display case, he would have grabbed it by its narrow neck, holding the pin upside down.

The Case of
the Mysterious Fire

LADIES AND GENTLEMEN OF THE JURY:

When a fire occurs, a question logically arises. Was the fire accidental or was it started on purpose, perhaps to collect insurance money?

That is the question presented to you today. Brenda Taylor, the plaintiff, seeks to collect insurance because her jewelry store was badly damaged by fire. Rightup Insurance Company refuses to pay the claim. The insurance company believes there is sufficient evidence to prove the fire was started on purpose.

Ms. Taylor is the owner of Jewelry Gems. The store had been in business for eight years. She gave the following testimony:

"I arrived at my store at the usual time, around 8:30 in the morning. As I put my key in the lock I could smell something burning. I opened the door and a burst of smoke hit me in the face.

"I screamed for help. Flames were creeping down from the ceiling. The smoke was so thick, I could barely see across the room.

"I hurried to save what I could. I emptied out a

63

drawer and began filling it with all the expensive jewelry I could find. But the smoke was too much. I could hardly breathe. That's when I ran outside. Just then, the fire truck arrived."

The fire captain said his station had received a phone call from an upstairs neighbor at 8:25 A.M. He met Brenda Taylor as she was running out of the store. She was gasping for breath.

As he took the drawer from her arms she collapsed on the sidewalk. The captain comforted Ms. Taylor while the men went inside.

A half hour later the fire was under control. But the damage was already done. The fire had been burning for hours. The display cases and shelves were badly damaged.

It was determined that weeks before the fire, Brenda Taylor had remodeled her store, purchased new display cases and more jewelry and installed a new lighting system. On the basis of its inspection, the fire department believes the fire broke out in the ceiling. But fire inspectors were unable to determine if defective wiring was the cause.

EXHIBIT A is the fire department report. It describes the heavy damage done by the fire.

EXHIBIT B is a photograph taken outside of the store minutes after the fire truck arrived. Thick smoke was still pouring out of the front of the jewelry store.

An investigator for the insurance company has explained to the court why his company refuses to pay the insurance claim. I quote from his statement:

"About two weeks before the fire, Brenda Taylor took out additional insurance with my company. She increased the amount by $30,000. We have determined that this amount was not justified by her remodeling costs or the additional things she purchased."

Rightup Insurance has entered as EXHIBIT C the new insurance policy.

The insurance investigator had looked into the financial affairs of Ms. Taylor and continued his testimony.

"My investigation shows that Ms. Taylor's business had fallen off about six months ago when a discount jewelry store opened down the street. In recent months, she twice missed payment of her rent.

"She told the landlord she could not afford to pay because business was so bad. According to the landlord, Brenda Taylor tried to break her rental lease, claiming the discount store was forcing her out of business.

"We further learned that Ms. Taylor had a meeting with a real estate agent in the next town. She told him she was interested in space to open a new store.

"We find it suspicious that Ms. Taylor would remodel her store while looking for a different location at the same time. We believe she did the remodeling as an excuse to increase the amount of her fire insurance.

"We find Brenda Taylor's actions highly questionable. It is our belief that Ms. Taylor was responsible for the fire in her jewelry store. She needed the insurance money to pay her debts.

"The fire also was a convenient excuse to move to a new location. Otherwise, why would she have been looking for a new store?

"In view of the excessive amount of Brenda Taylor's new insurance policy and her suspicious activities in the weeks prior to the fire, my company refuses to pay the claim."

LADIES AND GENTLEMEN OF THE JURY:
You have just heard the Case of the Mysterious Fire. You must decide the merits of Brenda Taylor's claim. Be sure to carefully examine the evidence in EXHIBITS A, B, and C.

Did the fire break out accidentally? Or did Brenda Taylor start it?

REPORT OF FIRE IN A BUILDING

Time of alarm __8:25 AM__   Date __JULY 3, 1987__

Discovered by __CARL FRANKS__

Building where fire started __JEWELRY GEMS__

__FIRST FLOOR AT 635 WALKER STREET__

Height (stories) __3__   Construction __BRICK__

Walls __BRICK__   Floor __WOOD__   Roof __PROTECTED__

Cause __UNKNOWN. POSSIBLY DEFECTIVE WIRING__

__IN CEILING__

Date property last inspected __JUNE 27, 1987__

Loss of life or injuries __NONE —__

__CONSIDERABLE DAMAGE TO CEILING AND__

__SHELVES, FURNITURE, ETC. SMOKE__

__DAMAGE TO WALLS.__

EXHIBIT C

EXHIBIT C

COMMERCIAL PROPERTY COVERAGE
DECLARATION PAGE

POLICY NO. 57216   EFFECTIVE DATE 6/16/87

NAME INSURED

Brenda Taylor
Jewelry Gems
635 Walker St. Flanders, Wisc.

DESCRIPTION OF PREMISES

First floor of brick, three-story bldg.

COVERAGE PROVIDED

PREM NO.	BLDG. NO.	COVERAGE	LIMIT OF INS.	COVERED CAUSES	CO. INS.	RATES
136	2	contents	$110,000	fire		$2,200
		improvements	25,000	fire		500
						$2,700

DEDUCTIBLE

NONE

VERDICT

THE FIRE WAS SET BY BRENDA TAYLOR.

EXHIBIT B shows the jewelry Brenda Taylor had thrown into the drawer before she ran out of the burning store. The boxes were neatly stacked, with the smaller ones on top of the larger ones. If she had hurried to fill it, the boxes would have been scattered in the drawer in no special order. Taylor packed the drawer with the jewelry *before* she set fire to the store. She left and returned to save the valuables when the fire began to rage.

The Case of
the Polluted River

LADIES AND GENTLEMEN OF THE JURY:

Pollution of the environment is a crime our society cannot allow. It endangers the quality of life both today and for future generations.

The State has accused Chemzon Industries of unlawfully dumping toxic waste in the waters of the Rhonda River. Chemzon Industries claims that it disposes of waste at its own safe dumping site and that the State's charges are unfounded.

The State called as its first witness Billy Lang, one of two boys who were floating on their raft down the Rhonda River.

"My friend and I had just built the raft. We thought it would be fun to have summer camping trips along the banks of the Rhonda.

"The day after school was over, we took our first trip. We set sail from the dock at Cedar Park. My friend was sunning himself and I was the navigator.

"We were drifting along for about fifteen minutes. I was looking into the water to see how far down I could see. All of a sudden I saw a dead fish float by our raft. As we drifted downstream, I spotted another dead fish and then another. Before I knew it, I saw pockets of them surfacing all around the raft.

"I grabbed one of the fish and pushed the raft toward shore. I thought the police should know what I found.

"As I neared shore, I saw this empty barrel floating in the water. My friend helped me pull it onto the raft."

EXHIBIT A is the cardboard barrel found by Billy Lang. The label clearly shows it contains Zendrite, a hazardous chemical. Markings on the barrel prove it is the property of Chemzon Industries.

Chemzon is a company that makes insecticides. The poisonous chemical, Zendrite, is a waste product that is left over after the insecticides have been made.

State law says that toxic chemical waste may not be dumped in any rivers. The law requires companies to get rid of their waste at special disposal sites.

The law was passed because companies were using the Rhonda River for dumping waste. Local fishermen complained that fishing conditions in the river had slowly become worse over the years. Before the law was passed, companies would drive trucks to an inlet along the river. They would empty barrels of chemicals into its waters. The barrel found by Billy Lang was floating near the river's inlet.

EXHIBIT B is a map of part of the Rhonda River. The location where Billy discovered the barrel is marked with an X.

Fred Chesterton, a vice president of Chemzon, was called to testify. First the question and then his answer:

Q: Has your company ever dumped chemicals into the Rhonda River?

A: Yes. We used to do it by the inlet like everyone else. There was a road leading to the water. That was before the State passed the new law. Now we take waste to our own disposal site.

Q: How often do you do this?

A: About every two weeks. Our own site is just outside of town.

EXHIBIT C is a photograph of the Chemzon waste site.

Q: Isn't it true that your waste site is nearly filled and your company has been trying to find land for a new one?

A: Yes. But we can still use our site for several months before it's full.

Q: How do you account for the barrel found in the Rhonda River?

A: I don't really know. It could have been an accident. Maybe when our truck was taking the waste from our plant to our dumping site, one of the barrels accidentally fell off the truck and rolled into the river. It could have floated to the inlet. Our loading dock is at the rear of the plant near the river.

Q: But the top of the barrel was missing. Aren't the barrels closed before they are loaded on your truck?

A: Yes they are. But it wouldn't take much for the top to fall off. We reuse the barrels and the tops don't always fit tightly.

The State feels that the death of the fish in the Rhonda River was not caused by a single barrel of chemicals. Rather, it was the result of frequent use of the river as a dumping ground. The State accuses Chemzon Industries of regularly dumping Zendrite into the water because their waste site was nearly full.

The State claims that while someone from Chemzon was pouring the toxic chemicals into the water by the inlet, the barrel accidentally fell into the river. It accuses Chemzon Industries of willfully violating the pollution law.

LADIES AND GENTLEMEN OF THE JURY:
You have just heard the Case of the Polluted River. You must decide the merit of the State's accusation.

Be sure to carefully examine the evidence in EXHIBITS A, B, and C.

Did Chemzon Industries purposely dump toxic waste into the Rhonda River? Or did the barrel accidentally fall off a truck at its plant?

EXHIBIT A

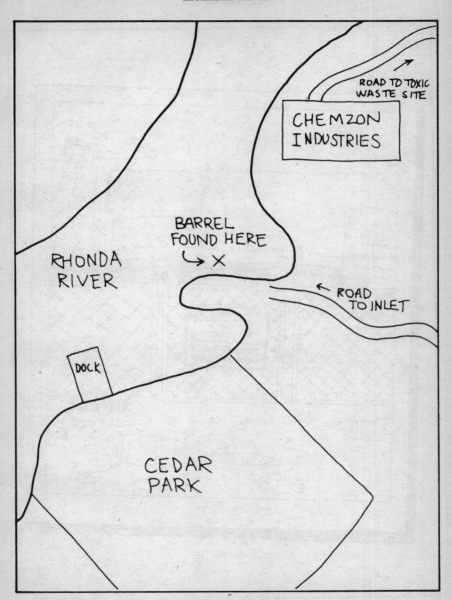

EXHIBIT C

VERDICT

CHEMZON INDUSTRIES IS GUILTY OF POLLUTION.

Billy Lang's raft was drifting downstream from the dock in Cedar Park, so the river was flowing in the direction *toward* Chemzon's plant. If the barrel had accidentally fallen off a truck at Chemzon's plant, it would have floated downstream, in the direction *away from* the inlet. Instead, the barrel was found floating near the inlet. It had fallen into the water at that location.

The Case of
the Broken Goldfish Bowl

Ladies AND GENTLEMEN OF THE JURY:

A person who is found at the scene of a crime is not necessarily a criminal.

Keep this in mind as you decide the case before you today.

The crime presented here today may seem unusual. No money or property was stolen. Rather, the act was one of outright vandalism in which someone purposely wrecked the rear room of the Pets-R-People Pet Shop.

James Bradley, the owner of the Pets-R-People Pet Shop, has accused Mike Webster of purposely wrecking the back room of the store. Mike Webster, a former employee of the store, claims he is innocent.

A night watchman has given the following testimony:

"It was on the night of August 17 that I was making my rounds at Concord Mall when I heard strange noises coming from the Pets-R-People Pet Shop. I tried the front door and found it unlocked. After contacting the owner, I entered the store.

"Nothing seemed unusual. I made my way to the rear. As I pulled apart the curtains leading to the back room, I was startled to find Mike Webster sprawled facedown on the floor.

"The rear room was a mess. Papers, bills, and files were torn and scattered throughout the room. Boxes were opened, their contents littered about. Piles of spilled pet food were all over the floor."

The watchman shook Webster and the man stirred. Half dazed, he rose to his feet.

Webster said he had gone to the pet store after it had closed because he had forgotten to feed the goldfish. While he was there, he heard the front door open. He called out, thinking it was the owner. Suddenly, he was rushed by a young teenage boy. Webster had never seen him before.

Webster was so frightened that he fainted, falling on the floor. This was the last he remembered until he was awakened by the night watchman. The police were called and they arrested Mike Webster.

James Bradley, the owner of Pets-R-People, testified as follows:

"Hey, I'm a nice guy, but Mike Webster was a terrible clerk. He often arrived late and spent time in the back room when he should have been helping customers.

"I finally had to talk to him about his poor performance. To my surprise, he started yelling and screaming at me that he worked as hard as he could. After that, I didn't want Webster to work in my store anymore. On the morning before the vandalism occurred, I notified Mike Webster by mail that he was fired. I was too scared to tell him to his face.

"You know what I think? I don't think there was any teenager who rushed in. I think it was Webster who wrecked the back room of my shop. I think he wanted to get back at me for firing him."

EXHIBIT A is the notice that was mailed to Webster. It was found in his pants pocket when he was arrested.

A lawyer for Mike Webster has given a different side of the story:

"Is James Bradley the nice guy he says he is? Or are there a lot of customers who might want to get even with him? It seems that Bradley has a history of improper store operation."

EXHIBIT B is a newspaper article which shows that James Bradley was ordered to close the previous pet shop he owned. During the time Bradley was operating his new store, he was sued three times by dissatisfied customers for selling them animals who turned out to be sickly. When the owners attempted to return the animals, Bradley refused to refund their money.

Mike Webster has given his side of the story:

"I think fish are the most beautiful animals in

the world, don't you? I have a big tank at home with dozens of little ones swimming around. Sure I was upset when I was fired. But it didn't stop me from caring for the goldfish in Mr. Bradley's store.

"I went back to the store that night because I had forgotten to feed the beautiful fish. When that crazy teenager rushed in, I just blacked out from fright."

Mike Webster's lawyer has entered into evidence EXHIBIT C, a photograph of the back room taken by the night watchman. You will note that as Webster fainted, he knocked over the fishbowl. The dead fish are lying near him.

The lawyer stated that if Webster had faked his fainting, he would never have knocked over the goldfish bowl as he pretended to fall. He was far too fond of fish.

Mike Webster's lawyer says his client is innocent. The damage was caused by an unknown teenage vandal who was an unhappy customer of the pet shop. His motive was to get back at Bradley for illegal business practices.

The lawyer for James Bradley claims that Mike Webster made up his story. He accuses Webster of pretending to faint when the night watchman was about to catch him wrecking the back room. There was no teenage vandal.

LADIES AND GENTLEMEN OF THE JURY:

You have just heard the Case of the Broken Goldfish Bowl. You must decide the merits of James Bradley's claim. Be sure to carefully examine the evidence in EXHIBITS A, B, and C.

Is Mike Webster guilty as charged? Or was the damage done by a teenage vandal?

EXHIBIT A

Pets-R-People
PET SHOP

Concord Mall
Cherry Valley, New Jersey

August 16, 1988

Dear Mr. Webster:

This letter is to inform you that, effective today, we are no longer in need of your services, and your employment has ceased immediately.

Your final paycheck is enclosed.

Sincerely,

James Bradley

James Bradley

Pets-R-People

Pet store owner fined, barred from business

The owner of a pet shop in town was ordered yesterday to close permanently his store.

A Superior Court Judge also ordered James Bradley to pay $15,000 in fines and about $5,000 to dissatisfied customers. Bradley had been convicted of various animal neglect charges.

Last month Bradley admitted violating several state consumer protection laws. He also admitted he did not provide pedigree papers to customers and that he failed to post proper consumer protection warnings.

The penalties imposed are in addition to those levied earlier this week by a judge who fined him for 100 animal cruelty violations.

(Story continued on page 8.)

EXHIBIT C

VERDICT

MIKE WEBSTER CAUSED THE DAMAGE.

Webster claimed he fainted when the teenager entered the back room. But EXHIBIT C shows he was lying *on top* of some of the papers. This would have been impossible unless the papers were on the floor *before he fell*—indicating it was Mike Webster who had vandalized the back room. He pretended to faint when the night watchman arrived.